First published 2006 by Walker Books Ltd, 87 Vauxhall Walk, London SE11 5HJ   This edition published 2016   2 4 6 8 10 9 7 5 3 1   This book has been typeset in Sharkey   Printed in China   © 2006 Niamh Sharkey   The right of Niamh Sharkey to be identified as author/illustrator of this work has been asserted by her in accordance with the Copyright, Designs and Patents Act 1988   This book has been typeset in Sharkey   All rights reserved. No part of this book may be reproduced, transmitted or stored in an information retrieval system in any form or by any means, graphic, electronic or mechanical, including photocopying, taping and recording, without prior written permission from the publisher.   British Library Cataloguing in Publication Data: a catalogue record for this book is available from the British Library   ISBN 978-1-4063-7119-2   www.walker.co.uk

For Oscar

THIS WALKER BOOK BELONGS TO:

_____

_____

_____

I'm a Happy Hugglewug

Niamh Sharkey

WALKER BOOKS
AND SUBSIDIARIES
LONDON • BOSTON • SYDNEY • AUCKLAND

My Hugglewug Song

Oh, oh, oh...
I'm a Hugglewug and I'm happy.
I jump in the air.
I've got twirly whirly horns
and spikey spikey hair.
I wriggle my fingers
and twiddle my toes.
Between my shiny shiny
eyes is my sniffy
sniffy nose.

My mouth is wibbly wobbly.

My tongue is this l... o... n... g...

My Hugglewug Family

My brother Cobby

Baby Ivor's teddy

My baby brother Ivor

My sister Lola

My mummy

My pet fish Horace

Me (Henry)

My daddy

My nanny

My grandaddy

Start the Day the Hugglewug Way!

Baby Ivor loves his porridge.

Gurgle wurgle

I love hugging Mummy.

Lola loves dancing after breakfast.

Cobby and Daddy love reading.

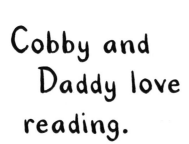

Come and Meet My Hugglewug Friends!

1, 2, 3,
we're off to school!

Hey! There's Oscar
chasing Denzel.
Go, go, guys

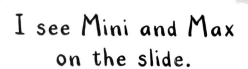

I see Mini and Max
on the slide.

Gertie is
skipping.

Bang that drum,
Ruby!

Jump over that
mushroom, Meg!

Splash! Splosh!
Stanley is in a puddle.

Tweet tweet

Miss Read
my teacher

I love
school too!

It's Time for Hugglewug School!

Here comes a Hugglewug through the window,

here comes a Hugglewug through the door.

Here comes a Hugglewug round the corner,

Hugglewugs! Hugglewugs! Hugglewugs! At Hugglewug School we learn to ...

The Scary Hugglewug Counting Game

1 Little

2 Little

4 Little

5 Little

7 Little

8 Little

9 Little Hugglewugs

3 Little Hugglewugs

6 Little Hugglewugs

10 Little Hugglewugs ...

CAN'T SCARE

ME!

Let's All Paint a Picture!

Splosh!

Look! Lola's dancing with a paintbrush.

Scribble!

Cobby is drawing a scary blue monster.

Squelch!

Ruby loves being messy.

Squirt!

Careful with that red paint, Denzel!

Climb the Hugglewug Tree!

It's after school — yippee yippee!
Time to play before our tea.

Whee!

Way hey!

Hugglewugs! Hugglewugs! Up a tree!
How many Hugglewugs can you see?

I Spy Hugglewug Pie

Muffin   Carrot   Hugglewug pie   Apple

Glass of
lemonade   Fork   Knife   Hugglebug

Worm

Spoon

Red
mushroom

Hugglewug
cake

Yellow
mushroom

Snail   Peas   Popcorn   Plate

Who Loves a Hugglewug?

Mummy
is so
squelchy!

Cobby
is so
huggly!

Daddy
is so
blobby!

Lola
is so
wuggly!

I'm so
snuggly!

Baby
is so
Hugglewuggly!

My Hugglewug Lullaby

I see the moon,
the moon sees me.

Hugglewug moon!
Hugglewug me!

Let's Sing Again!

Oh, oh, oh...

I'm a Hugglewug
and I'm happy.
I jump
in the air.

I've got twirly whirly horns

and spikey spikey hair.

I wriggle my fingers

and twiddle my toes.

Between my shiny shiny eyes is my sniffy sniffy nose.

My mouth is wibbly wobbly.

My tongue is this l... o... n... g...

S. Come on, everybody!
Sing our Hugglewug Song!

Oh, oh, oh...

WALKER BOOKS is the world's leading
independent publisher of children's books.
Working with the best authors and illustrators
we create books for all ages, from babies
to teenagers – books your child will
grow up with and always remember. So…

FOR THE BEST CHILDREN'S BOOKS, LOOK FOR THE BEAR